Soraya
the Skiing
Fairy

By Daisy Meadows

ORCHARD

www.orchardseriesbooks.co.uk

Fairyland Palace

Surfing Festival

Port Pearl Beach

Youth Hostel

Skate Park

Jack Frost's Ode

Each goody-goody fairy pest
Says 'Never cheat' and 'Try your best'.
Their words should end up in the bin.
To be the best you have to win!

I'll steal and cheat to find a way
Of winning every game I play,
And when the world is at my feet
They'll see it's always best to cheat!

Contents

Chapter One
Dewbelle Resort

It was early morning in the Mistfall Mountains. The rising sun beamed down on a large wooden chalet at the edge of a snowy pine forest. Shafts of sunlight pierced the gaps in the curtains.

Kirsty Tate sat up in bed, rubbing her eyes. She looked around and smiled.

"Even the morning light looks different here," she said.

Her best friend, Rachel Walker, leaned over the edge of the top bunk and smiled down at her.

"Mum says that Dewbelle is the prettiest resort in Silverlake Valley," she said. "She worked here when she was a teenager."

Kirsty threw back her thick quilt and Rachel half-jumped down the bunk-bed ladder. Together, they pulled back the curtains and flung open the window. A cold, crisp scent filled the little room. Outside, the freshly fallen snow looked as smooth as icing. It had been dark when they arrived the night before. Now they could see far beyond the ski slopes of Dewbelle, to where the Mistfall Mountains rose in the distance.

"The snow looks perfect," said Kirsty. "We could build a million snowmen."

Rachel laughed.

"We're going to be too busy learning how to ski," she said. "I can't wait to get started. I just hope that Jack Frost doesn't spoil the fun."

It was six months since the summer

Gold Medal Games, when lots of children from different schools had come together to learn how to surf and skateboard. Now it was time for the winter games. Kirsty gazed at the ski slopes in silence.

"Are you OK?" asked Rachel, giving her a friendly nudge.

"I can't help thinking about what Jack Frost said in the summer," Kirsty replied. "He said that winter was *his* time. He's had months to plan something really horrible."

During the summer competition, Rachel and Kirsty had shared a wonderful adventure. Jack Frost had stolen the magical items that belonged to the Gold Medal Fairies. Calling himself Lightning Jack of the Frost Academy, he had tried to win the competitions by cheating. Rachel and Kirsty had helped to foil his plans, but he still had two of the magical items.

"He's never defeated the fairies, and he never will," said Rachel. "Let's go and have breakfast. This mountain air is making me hungry."

All the competitors were staying in the same chalet. As soon as they were dressed, they hurried down the wooden stairs. Two boys and a girl joined them on the way, and Rachel and Kirsty introduced themselves.

"I'm Valentina," said the girl. "This is Lenny…"

"And I'm Lee Vee," said the blonde boy. "This place is amazing, isn't it? I can't wait to try snowboarding."

"Be patient, we're learning to ski first," said Valentina, grinning.

They arrived at the dining room and found two long wooden tables with benches on either side. Several children were already tucking into breakfast. There was an open kitchen at the far end of the room, where a young woman in a white outfit was standing at the cooker. She was stirring various pots and pans, while a young man dashed back and forth, delivering plates of sausages, piles of hot toast, bowls of porridge, and jugs of milk, orange juice and water.

"Wow," said Rachel. "Just looking at this makes my tummy rumble."

They sat down at the end of a bench and the young man darted over to them.

"Hi, guys," he said with a broad smile. "My name's Ty, and that's Kim over in the kitchen."

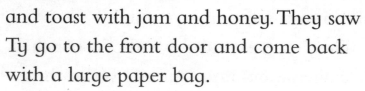

"Do you own the chalet?" asked Kirsty.

"No," said Ty with a laugh. "I'm your host, ski teacher and waiter all rolled into one. So what can I get you for breakfast?"

Soon Rachel, Kirsty and their new friends were enjoying porridge, boiled eggs, and toast with jam and honey. They saw Ty go to the front door and come back with a large paper bag.

"Croissants," he explained when he saw them looking. "The local bakery delivers them warm and fresh every morning."

"Oh my goodness, my tummy just rumbled again," said Rachel, laughing.

Kim opened the bag and frowned.

"There aren't enough," she said, sounding confused. "The bakery never makes mistakes."

"There were some funny footprints in the snow beside the bag," said Ty. "Perhaps someone took them."

"Let's share the croissants so we can all have a taste," Valentina suggested.

Everyone agreed, and Rachel and Kirsty exchanged a quick glance.

"Strange footprints and stolen food?" said Kirsty under her breath. "That sounds like goblins!"

Chapter Two
Tree Slalom

Rachel and Kirsty finished eating quickly and slipped away from the dining room. They pulled on their boots, hats and scarves, and opened the front door. Three sets of large, big-toed footprints criss-crossed each other and led away from the chalet. Flaky crumbs were scattered

across the footprints.

"Croissant crumbs!" said Kirsty
excitedly. "The footprints are heading
towards the forest."

"Let's follow them," said Rachel.

They sank into the snow as they
walked beside the prints. At the edge of
the forest, the prints swerved towards the
ski slopes and the lifts.

Rachel started to follow them, but Kirsty didn't move. She was staring up at one of the pine trees. Every snowy branch was glowing.

"Magic," she whispered.

"There's something moving!" Rachel exclaimed.

A tiny figure appeared, squealing with delight as she dropped and skidded from branch to snowy branch in her ski boots. She was wearing red ski trousers, with a red-and-pink top and a matching helmet. Her brown hair gleamed in the sunlight.

"It's Soraya the Skiing Fairy!" said Kirsty.

"Hi Rachel, hi Kirsty," said Soraya, panting and laughing.

She skidded to a stop and a little burst of snow sprinkled down on to the girls.

"Snow is fun
even without my
skis," she said, "But
I have mountains
of energy and
swinging through
trees isn't enough to
burn it off. I have
to find my skis."

"It's great that
you're here," said
Rachel. "We've just
seen some goblin
footprints."

"If you turn us into fairies, we could
follow them," Kirsty suggested.

"Not a chance," said Soraya, to their
surprise. "You can't miss out on your first
skiing lesson!"

She zoomed into Rachel's hood.

"Come on," she said "It's ski time!"

Back at the chalet, the other competitors were collecting their skis and getting into their skiing clothes. Kirsty and Rachel found theirs quickly, and then they noticed Valentina. She was standing still as everyone else was pulling on their jackets, hats and goggles. Tears were welling up in her eyes.

"Valentina, what's wrong?" Kirsty asked.

"I can't find my things," Valentina said in a small voice.

Rachel put her arm around Valentina's shoulders.

"We can help," she said. "I've got a spare helmet you can borrow."

"You can use my spare goggles," said Lee Vee.

"I've got another jacket that'll fit you," said Kirsty.

Other people started to offer their spares too. Between them, they soon came up with a full outfit for Valentina. Rachel heard a tiny tapping sound, and guessed that Soraya was clapping her hands together.

"This is exactly what skiing is all

about," she whispered. "Having a blast with friends, and no one being left out."

Ty showed them how to carry their skis and then led them all to the beginner slope, where a small section had been reserved just for them.

"This is where we're going to hang out this morning," he said.

Rachel and Kirsty looked around. There were already lots of new skiers on the slopes, sliding along on wobbly legs or falling into powdery pillows of snow.

"I hope I can do it," said Kirsty.

"You're going to love it," said Soraya.

Soraya was right. Ty explained how to click their ski boots into their skis. First he showed them how to slide. Then he taught them how to do a snowplough, which was a way of stopping by moving the tips of their skis together.

"Great snowplough!" he cheered as Kirsty managed to stop without falling over.

"Great landing!" he chuckled when Rachel fell onto her bottom, laughing.

"This is the best fun," said Rachel as she stood up. "I've never tried a sport where going wrong felt so right!"

"Winter sports are awesome," said Ty, skiing among them and giving advice.

"You've got four days of mountain fun ahead, thanks to the Gold Medal Games. Today you'll be learning to ski, and tomorrow there's a competition where you can try out your new skills. This is your chance to experience sports you've never tried before, so give it your best shot."

Just then, three boys tramped across the snow to join them. They were wearing green ski suits, green helmets and green goggles. Their ski boots were enormous.

"You're a bit late, guys," said Ty, glancing at his watch. "Let's get you into your skis."

Rachel and Kirsty stared at the boys and then exchanged a little nod.

"Soraya," Kirsty whispered. "Here come the goblins!"

Chapter Three
Green Skiers

At first, the three goblins listened to Ty and did what he said.

"Maybe they really want to learn to ski," said Rachel.

They carried on practising. Soraya kept calling out advice from inside Rachel's hood, and soon the girls were hardly falling over at all. Ty clapped his hands together and everyone slid over to him.

"You're all doing really well," he said. "I think it's time to have a go on the drag lift. This is a really simple way of getting up the slope. All you have to do is hold on and let it pull you."

He showed them how to hold on to a pole and let it drag them up to the top of the slope.

"Me first," said the tallest goblin, shoving his way to the front.

He started up the slope, followed by the other two goblins.

"OK," said Ty, looking surprised by their rudeness. "You saw them do it. Now it's your turn. Don't be afraid. Remember to hold on tight."

Lenny held his ski poles in one hand

and grabbed the lift pole with the other.

"Hey, what's going on?" he exclaimed.

The lift pole shuddered and jerked. Lee was shaken off and thrown into the snow.

"You boys," Ty shouted. "Stop that!"

At the top of the slope, the goblins were swinging on the large wheel that pulled the lift up. They were making the poles of the drag lift leap around as if they were dancing. Ty, frowning, started to climb up the slope sideways on his skis.

"That'll take ages," Soraya whispered. "A little magic would be quicker…"

Glancing around, Rachel and Kirsty dived out of sight behind a fence. Soraya slipped out of Rachel's hood and shook her wand, sending glittering snowflakes over the girls. Each one glowed as it landed, and a delicious warmth spread

through their bodies. In a flurry of icy
sparkles, they shrank to fairy size. The
snowflakes had turned their clothes and
helmets white, and petal-like wings
carried them into the air. The goblins
were still jerking the lift and squawking
with laughter.

"No one will see us now we're so small," said Rachel.

"Come on," said Soraya, zooming towards the lift.

Rachel and Kirsty were close behind her. The cold air stung their cheeks as they sped up the slope.

"Jack Frost must have ordered them to do this," said Kirsty.

"Let's ask them," said Soraya, landing on the wheel and folding her arms. "Goblins, are you following naughty orders again?"

The goblins yelled in shock and let go of the wheel.

"Leave us alone," shouted the tallest goblin as he skied away down the slope.

"Pesky fairies," yelled the other two, following him down.

Soraya quickly turned the girls back
into humans again and they rejoined the
others.

By lunchtime, everyone in the group
was sliding confidently down the
beginner slope and able to stop on both
sides.

"Let's grab something to eat," said Ty.
"Then I think you can take on a bigger
challenge."

He led them to a café at the bottom of
the slope. There were lots of large tables
outside so they could enjoy the winter
sunshine as they ate. Soon the tables were
filled with bowls of chips, fresh salads and
jugs of squash.

"May I have a chip?" Soraya
whispered. "All this mountain air makes
me absolutely starving."

Kirsty pushed a chip under her hair and felt Soraya take it. Rachel glimpsed the little fairy eating the chip like a giant corn on the cob.

"I would love to eat a chip that's bigger than me," she said, giggling.

Suddenly, a loud, boastful voice rang

out above the chatter.

"Out of my way! Make some noise for the best skier in the Mistfall Mountains!"

Chapter Four
The Ghost of Spider Pickles

Jack Frost came striding between the tables, holding a magnificent pair of red skis.

"Yes, you can believe your eyes," he said, nodding around at everyone. "Lightning Jack from the Frost Academy really is here. No autographs, please."

He stomped over to where the goblins were sitting.

"Has he got my magical skis?" Soraya whispered in breathless excitement. "I don't dare look in case he spots me."

"They're red," said Rachel.

"If they're mine, they will have my name on the bottom in swirly writing," Soraya told them.

The girls craned their necks and peered at the skis in Jack Frost's hand. Sure enough, Soraya's name was written on each one.

"Yes, we found them!" Kirsty said, high-fiving Rachel. "But how are we going to get them back?"

Rachel tugged on Kirsty's arm and they slipped down under the table. From here, it was easy to crawl along until they reached the goblins. They crouched beside three pairs of spindly goblin legs and listened.

"Why are the humans still smiling?" Jack Frost was demanding. "I told you to make them miserable."

"We tried stealing their clothes, but that didn't work," said the tallest goblin.

"We tried to break the lift, but that didn't work," added the second goblin.

"They have fun even when they're falling over," said the third goblin.

"Listen to me, nincompoops," Jack Frost hissed. "I want those Gold Medal competitors to have such a miserable time that they don't even want to be in the competition tomorrow."

"I thought you said you'd win easily," said the tallest goblin.

"I *will*!" Jack Frost snarled at him. "I'm just making extra sure, that's all."

Soraya flew out and hovered under the table, glaring upwards.

"I wish I could go out there and give him a piece of my mind," she uttered. "Oh girls, we *have* to get my skis back or tomorrow will be a disaster."

Just then, Ty stood up and grinned at them all.

"Now lunch is over, let's try a trickier slope," he said. "The colour of a slope tells you how difficult it is. You've been on a green slope this morning. Blue is the next stage up, followed by red and black."

"Will it be very fast?" said Kirsty, feeling a tingle of fear.

"It's faster than a green slope," said Ty. "But I know you can handle this. Be brave, and you're sure to love it."

"Great advice," said Soraya. "I'm longing to get my skis back on my feet."

Just then, Rachel noticed that the goblins were huddled together. They were whispering and nodding eagerly.

"They're up to something," she said.

Ty led everyone to the chair lifts and explained what they had to do.

"Remember," he said. "When you reach the top of the slope, just lean forwards and slide out of your chair. Let your skis take you!"

Lenny and Lee Vee were first. They sat side by side in each chair and were carried upwards, their legs dangling high above the slope. The other children followed, laughing as they lurched up into the air. Kirsty and Rachel were last in the queue.

"Oh my goodness,"

squeaked Rachel as the chair jerked forwards. "I definitely prefer flying."

"You can do this," Soraya whispered.

As the chair swooped towards the top of the slope, the girls leaned forwards and slid down the slope.

"Excellent," said Ty when they reached the bottom.

They joined the queue again. But this time, something was different. The chair lifts were swaying more than before.

"Do the lifts look faster to you?" Kirsty asked.

"They *are* faster!" Soraya exclaimed from under Kirsty's hair. "There will be an accident if they don't slow down."

"Our new friends are up there," said Rachel. "We have to do something."

Kirsty looked around and saw a little

hut at the bottom of the slope. The wires of the chair lift were attached to it.

"Maybe the controls are in there," she said.

She zoomed down to the hut with Rachel close behind her. Through the single, open window, they saw…

"Goblins!" Rachel exclaimed.

The three goblins were hunched over the lift controls. The tallest goblin had one bony finger pressed on the 'speed' button.

"How can we get them to stop?" Kirsty whispered.

Just then, the smallest goblin looked up and shivered. Hundreds of cobwebs filled the roof space.

"D-do you think there are s-spiders here?" he asked. "I don't like s-spiders."

Kirsty grinned and cupped her hands around her mouth.

"I am the ghost of Spider Pickles," she said in a hollow voice. "Leave this hut or feel my tickles!"

The goblins stared at each other with open mouths. Then…

"ARGHHH!"

47

Squawking in fear, they shot out of the hut and disappeared over a snow bank. Rachel and Kirsty let out long sighs of relief as the chair lift slowed down. For now, Jack Frost's plan had been foiled.

Chapter Five
Goblin Slalom

After a full day of skiing, the girls spent
a restless night dreaming of goblins and
green slopes. Soraya slept in Kirsty's
chunky bobble hat, and in the morning
she tucked herself inside its turned-up
brim. It was time for the competition.

Ty showed them a blue run that had

been marked with yellow ribbon and poles.

"This is the slalom for today," he said. "Slalom is the special name for the competition slope. The markers show you which way to go. Remember, it's not just about who is the fastest. The judges are looking for good technique. Be at the start line at ten o'clock. Good luck, everyone, and have fun!"

There was time for a practice run before the competition, so Rachel and Kirsty headed to the top of the slope. The three goblins were there in their ski gear, waving their arms at each other. As the girls watched, the tallest one bonked another on the head with his ski pole.

"They're quarrelling," said Kirsty, moving closer.

"I've already got them on," the middle-sized goblin was squawking. "Me first."

"But *I* sneaked them away from Jack Frost while he was snoring," the tallest one whined.

"Oh, he's going to be so cross with us," moaned the smallest goblin, wringing his bony hands.

"Shut up, scaredy cat," sneered the first goblin. "We can return the skis before he even knows we borrowed them. Anyway, he told us to come and spoil things for the humans. We've followed his orders, and now it's time for fun."

He stamped one foot, and the girls saw a flash of red.

"He's got my skis!" exclaimed Soraya.

"He's taken them from Jack Frost," said Rachel. "This is our chance to get them back."

"Oh my goodness," said Kirsty. "What *are* they doing?"

Two of the goblins had taken their ordinary skis off and were now climbing onto the back of the middle-sized goblin. Wobbling violently, he bent his knees and leaned forwards.

SWOOSH! In a second all three of them were shooting down the slope, swaying wildly from side to side and yelling at the tops of their voices.

"Make way!"

"Top skiers coming through!"

Competitors dived left and right to get out of their way, landing face down in the heaped snow

at the side of the slope.

"They're out of control!" cried Kirsty.

Losing their balance, the goblins windmilled their arms, toppled over a snow bank and vanished from sight.

"Come on!" Rachel exclaimed.

They clicked out of their skis and scrambled down the bank into a small thicket of trees. The snow was deep here, and it was hard to walk in their heavy ski boots.

"Listen," said Soraya, fluttering out of Kirsty's hat brim. "I can hear something."

A large pile of snow nearby suddenly trembled. Rachel and Kirsty crouched down behind a tree as the three goblins burst out, shaking snow from their large ears.

"That was the stupid human's fault," grumbled the middle-sized goblin, yanking Soraya's skis out of the snow.

"I don't like it here," said the tallest goblin. "There are too many silly humans getting in the way."

"I wish we could have our own competition back at home in Goblin Grotto," said the smallest goblin longingly.

"We can!" squawked the middle-sized goblin. "We've done what Jack Frost said – we've messed up the track markers. Let's take these magical skis and set up a ski run at home."

Bickering about who would go first in their competition, the goblins clambered away. Rachel and Kirsty stood up, and Soraya hovered in front of them.

"There's no time to lose," she said. "We have to follow them to Goblin Grotto."

She raised her wand and a silvery light

made the thicket shine. It grew brighter and more dazzling, pressing in on them from all sides, until they were at the centre of a shining bubble. They felt themselves turning into fairies again as the silvery bubble of light carried them up, higher and higher. Soon the treetops and the mountains looked like a tiny map far below.

"We're going into a cloud," said Kirsty, looking up.

White mist swirled around the bubble, and then they started to sink. The bubble drifted downwards and they saw a collection of higgledy-piggledy roofs below.

"Goblin Grotto," Rachel whispered.

The goblin village looked just the same, but the snowy hills around it were very

different. Strings of colourful fairy lights
marked out ski runs. Crowds of goblins
were standing around the slopes. There
were goblins carrying little trays, selling
snacks, drinks and souvenir keyrings.
There were judges and photographers.
The three goblins from Dewbelle were
standing at the top of the slope, grinning

from ear to ear. The middle-sized goblin was wearing the red skis.

"The goblins have been busy using my magic," said Soraya.

The bubble carried them to the bottom of the slope and burst with a gentle pop. Rachel, Kirsty and Soraya fluttered down to hide behind an icy mound.

"We need a plan," said Kirsty. "We have to get those skis back."

"How can we get close with all those goblins watching?" Rachel asked.

There was a loud crack and a roaring shout, followed by a lot of goblin squawks and squeals. Carefully, the three fairies peeped over the top of the icy mound.

Jack Frost was standing at the top of the slope, and he looked *furious*.

Chapter Six
Race Against Time

"Give them back!" Jack Frost yelled, pointing at the red skis.

In terror, the middle-sized goblin jumped, slipped and hurtled backwards down the slope, letting out a wail like a fire engine.

"Idiot!" Jack Frost howled.

He started to pound down the slope after the goblin, shaking his fist. It was slow going, because he sank deeper into the snow with each step.

"Watch out!" cried Soraya.

The goblin was heading straight towards them. He hit the snow bank, flew into the air, performed an amazing triple twist and landed facing the fairies.

"Oof!" he said, and fell onto his bottom.

Rachel looked up at the slope. Jack Frost was getting closer, and an idea popped into her head.

"We don't have long," she said to the goblin. "You can't keep the skis. Either you let Jack Frost take them, or you give them back to their rightful owner."

"That's not fair," the goblin wailed. "I want to keep the ski slope."

"If Soraya had her skis back, she could keep the slope as it is," said Rachel.

"That's true," said Soraya. "I could add more runs and even a little mountain café that serves your favourite food."

"Frosty fungus flavoured jelly beans and bogmallows," said the goblin, licking his lips. "Yummy. It's a deal."

He unclicked the skis, picked them up and handed them to Soraya. As soon as she touched them, they glowed.

"Thank you," said Soraya.

She clicked her boots into the skis and then sprang out of her hiding place, coming face to face with Jack Frost.

"Take those off!" he snarled.

"The Gold Medal Games will be a success," Soraya said. "It's obvious that you love skiing. Why not stay here and

have fun competing with the goblins?"

"Competitions aren't about fun, you feather-brained fairy," he yelled. "Winning is the only thing that matters."

Rachel and Kirsty flew out too.

"You're wrong," said Kirsty. "Please try to see how much fun you can have just by taking part."

"Rubbish," Jack Frost retorted. "I'll show you all. I've still got the magical snowboard, and I'm going to be the best snowboarder in the world."

In a crackle of blue lightning, he had gone. Soraya turned to the girls.

"I'm going to stay here and teach the goblins how to have a safe and happy competition," she said. "When you get back to Dewbelle, everything will be back as it should be."

"Thank you," said Rachel. "I can't wait to take part."

"Thank *you*," said Soraya, with a flash of her beaming smile. "It's because of you that I can put everything right."

She threw her arms around them and they shared a big, squeezy hug. Then she flicked her wand, and snow surrounded the girls in a swirl of white. Seconds later they were back in the thicket of trees in Dewbelle. Kirsty checked her watch.

"It's past ten o'clock," she said. "Come on, we're late for the competition."

They climbed back up the bank, found their skis and zoomed down to the start of the slalom. Ty and the other children waved to them.

"Everyone wanted to wait until you got here," Ty told them, grinning. "They wouldn't start the competition until everyone was here. That's the true spirit of winter sports."

It was a wonderful morning. One by one, each competitor skied down through the clearly marked tracks to the finishing line. The crowd cheered and clapped. Cameras flashed, TV presenters chattered and happy music blared out. By the time it was their turn, Rachel and Kirsty were hoarse from whooping.

"Let's go together," said Rachel suddenly. "I know we're supposed to do it alone, but I want to share every moment with you."

Kirsty nodded, beaming, and they skied down side by side. The crowd applauded as they kept in perfect time and stopped in a spray of snow at the bottom.

"Great stuff," said Ty, clapping his hands as he walked towards them. "I've never seen new skiers work together like that before. You must be really good friends."

"The best," said Kirsty.

When everyone had finished, the head judge stood up.

"We have been very impressed with all the performances today," she announced.

"A special mention has to go to Kirsty Tate of Wetherbury School and Rachel Walker of Tippington School, who worked together to give us an unexpected double ski run."

There was a burst of applause, and the girls shared a smile.

"However, there can only be one winner. This year's gold medal for skiing is awarded to Valentina Vale of Allenross Academy."

The crowd cheered and whooped as Valentina went up to collect her award.

"Thank you," she said, sounding a little nervous. "This is amazing. I feel as if the medal should be shared between all of us. Learning to ski has been so much fun, and without my friends helping me yesterday, I wouldn't have been able to join in."

Everyone cheered again. Rachel linked arms with Kirsty.

"Now there is only Jayda's snowboard left to find," she said.

"Lightning Jack sounds determined to win," said Kirsty.

"Whatever happens, one thing's for certain," said Rachel. "He can't break the spirit of the Gold Medal Games!"

The End

Now it's time for Kirsty and
Rachel to help...

Jayda the Snowboarding Fairy

Read on for a sneak peek...

"WOW!"

Rachel Walker whooped as a
snowboarder sped down the biggest slope
in the snowboard park.

"Do you think we'll ever be able to do
that?" said her best friend, Kirsty Tate.

"I hope so," said Rachel, crossing her
fingers. "It looks like lots of fun."

It was Rachel and Kirsty's third day
in Dewbelle Resort in the Mistfall
Mountains. Together with a group of
children from various schools, they
had been taking part in the Gold
Medal Games since last summer. The

snowboarding competition was the last event of the season.

"Don't worry," said their snowboarding instructor, Kim. "We were all beginners once. The best thing you can do is relax and have fun."

The board park was next to the main ski slope, and it was filled with snowboarders doing the best kicks, flicks and tricks the girls had ever seen. They were sliding on slopes, half pipes and even picnic tables.

"Awesome!" exclaimed Valentina, who had won the skiing gold medal the day before.

She was gazing at a snowboarder who had just done a full somersault in mid-air. He was dressed in ice blue, and his white helmet had an ice-blue lightning bolt on its side. His board was also white and blue, and it was decorated with pink and yellow flowers.

"That's Lightning Jack," said Joe, a boy from Kirsty's school. "He's amazing. I've been watching him."

Read Jayda the Snowboarding Fairy to find out what adventures are in store for Kirsty and Rachel!

Read the brand-new series
from Daisy Meadows...

Ride. Dream. Believe.

Meet best friends Aisha and Emily
and journey to the secret world of
Enchanted Valley!

Calling all parents, carers and teachers!
The Rainbow Magic fairies are here to help
your child enter the magical world of reading.
Whatever reading stage they are at, there's
a Rainbow Magic book for everyone!
Here is Lydia the Reading Fairy's guide to
supporting your child's journey at all levels.

Starting Out

1 Our Rainbow Magic Beginner Readers are perfect for first-time readers who are just beginning to develop reading skills and confidence. Approved by teachers, they contain a full range of educational levelling, as well as lively full-colour illustrations.

Developing Readers

2 Rainbow Magic Early Readers contain longer stories and wider vocabulary for building stamina and growing confidence. These are adaptations of our most popular Rainbow Magic stories, specially developed for younger readers in conjunction with an Early Years reading consultant, with full-colour illustrations.

Going Solo

3 The Rainbow Magic chapter books - a mixture of series and one-off specials - contain accessible writing to encourage your child to venture into reading independently. These highly collectible and much-loved magical stories inspire a love of reading to last a lifetime.

www.orchardseriesbooks.co.uk

"Rainbow Magic got my daughter reading chapter books. Great sparkly covers, cute fairies and traditional stories full of magic that she found impossible to put down" - Mother of Edie (6 years)

"Florence LOVES the Rainbow Magic books. She really enjoys reading now" - Mother of Florence (6 years)

Read along the Reading Rainbow!

Well done – you have completed the book!

This book was worth 1 star.

See how far you have climbed on the Reading Rainbow opposite.
The more books you read, the more stars you can colour in
and the closer you will be to becoming a Royal Fairy!

Do you want to print your own Reading Rainbow?

1) Go to the Rainbow Magic website

2) Download and print out the poster

3) Colour in a star for every book you finish
and climb the Reading Rainbow

4) For every step up the rainbow,
you can download your very own certificate

There's all this and lots more at
orchardseriesbooks.co.uk

You'll find activities, stories, a special newsletter
AND you can search for the fairy with your name!